A Note to Parents and Caregivers:

With a focus on math, science, and social studies, *Read-it!* Readers support both the learning of content information and the extension of more complex reading skills. They encourage the development of problem-solving skills that help children expand their thinking.

 The PURPLE LEVEL presents basic topics and objects using high frequency words and simple language patterns.

 The RED LEVEL presents familiar topics using common words and repeating sentence patterns.

 The BLUE LEVEL presents new ideas using a larger vocabulary and varied sentence structure.

 The YELLOW LEVEL presents more challenging ideas, a broad vocabulary, and wide variety in sentence structure.

 The GREEN LEVEL presents more complex ideas, an extended vocabulary range, and expanded language structures.

 The ORANGE LEVEL presents a wide range of ideas and concepts using challenging vocabulary and complex language structures.

When sharing a content focused book with your child, read to find out facts and concepts, pausing often to restate and talk about the new information. The realistic story format provides an opportunity to talk about the language used, and to learn about reading to problem-solve for information. Encourage children to measure, make maps, and consider other situations that allow them to apply what they are learning.

There is no right or wrong way to share books with children. Find time to read and share new learning with your child, and pass on the legacy of literacy.

Adria F. Klein, Ph.D.
Professor Emeritus
California State University
San Bernardino, California

Editor: Jill Kalz
Designer: Tracy Davies
Page Production: Melissa Kes
Art Director: Nathan Gassman
Associate Managing Editor: Christianne Jones
The illustrations in this book were created with acrylics and collage.

Picture Window Books
151 Good Counsel Drive
P.O. Box 669
Mankato, MN  56002-0669
877-845-8392
www.picturewindowbooks.com

Printed in the United States of America.

All books published by Picture Window Books
are manufactured with paper containing at least
10 percent post-consumer waste.

**Library of Congress Cataloging-in-Publication Data**
Shaskan, Trisha Speed, 1973–
Fair game / by Trisha Speed Shaskan ; illustrated by Erik Christenson.
p. cm. — (Read-it! readers: character education)
ISBN 978-1-4048-4233-5 (library binding)
ISBN 978-1-4048-4237-3 (paperback)
[1. Basketball—Fiction. 2. Sportsmanship—Fiction. 3. Youths' art.]
I. Christenson, Erik, 1985– ill. II. Title.
PZ7.S53242Fag 2008
[E]—dc22                                    2008007168

# FAIR GAME

by Trisha Speed Shaskan
illustrated by Erik Christenson

Special thanks to our advisers for their expertise:

Kay A. Augustine, ED.S.
National Character Development Trainer and Consultant

Adria F. Klein, Ph.D.
Professor Emeritus, California State University
San Bernardino, California

PiCTURE WiNDOW BOOKS
Minneapolis, Minnesota

Ty, Diego, and Chris played basketball together at the gym after school.

Chris liked to dribble. He dribbled the
ball between his legs and behind his back.

5

Diego liked to shoot. He made layups and free throws. He even shot three-pointers.

Ty liked to pass. He passed the ball
around his back. He had great timing.
When Diego was open, Ty passed him
the ball so he could make the shot.

7

On Monday, a new boy came to the gym.
"My name is Jude," he said. "Can I play?"
"Sure," said Chris.

Jude couldn't dribble as well as Chris. He couldn't shoot as well as Diego. He couldn't pass as well as Ty. But he tried hard. He made the boys laugh by making up nicknames.

When Chris dribbled the ball between his long legs, Jude called him "Ostrich."

When Diego made a three-pointer, the ball fell through the net and bounced back. Jude called Diego "Boomerang."

When Ty passed the ball so quickly that it blurred, Jude called him "Lightning."

Chris, Diego, and Ty liked Jude and the funny nicknames he made up.

On Tuesday, Chris, Diego, and Ty were happy when Jude showed up at the gym.

"Want to play two on two?" Chris asked.

"Sounds great," said Jude.

"We finally have enough players," said Ty.

"Let's play!" said Diego.

Diego guarded Ty. Jude guarded Chris.
When Chris dribbled, Jude slapped his hand
and stole the ball.

"Hey, Jude, stop fouling,"
said Chris. "Play fair."

The next day, Chris said, "I don't want to play against Jude."

"Come on," said Diego. "It'll be fun."

14

This time, Chris guarded Ty. Jude guarded Diego. When Diego shot a three-pointer, Jude jumped up. He blocked the shot and crashed into Diego.

"Hey, Jude, stop fouling," said Diego. "Play fair."

On Thursday, Diego said, "I don't want to play against Jude."

"Me, neither," said Chris.

This time, Diego guarded Chris. Jude guarded Ty.

When Ty passed the ball to Chris, Jude lunged for the ball. He elbowed Diego.

"Hey, Jude, stop fouling," said Ty. "Play fair."

On Friday, Ty said, "I don't want to play with you, Jude."

"Me, neither," said Chris.

"Me, neither," said Diego.

"I'm just playing defense," said Jude.

"That's not defense," said Ty.

"You always foul," said Chris.

"You don't play fair," said Diego. "We don't want to play with you anymore."

Jude sadly walked off the basketball court and went home.

The next week, Ty said,
"Now that Jude's gone,
we'll have to play two
against one."

"Since you're
the best shot,
Diego, maybe
you should play
alone," said Chris.

"I'll try," said Diego.

Diego tried to shoot a three-pointer. But he couldn't make the shot with Ty and Chris both guarding him. He wished Jude were there to help him. He missed hearing Jude call him "Boomerang."

"This isn't fair," said Diego.
"I can't play against both
of you."

"It can't be that
bad," said Ty.

"You try," said Diego.

Ty dribbled the ball. But he didn't have anyone to pass it to. He wished Jude were there to catch a pass. He missed hearing Jude call him "Lightning."

Instead, Chris stole the ball, and Diego shot it in.

"This isn't fair," said Ty. "I can't play against both of you, either."

"I'll try," said Chris.

Chris dribbled by Diego. But Ty stopped him. Chris was outnumbered. He wished Jude were there to help him. He missed hearing Jude call him "Ostrich."

"This isn't working,"
said Chris.

"It's not as fun without
Jude," Diego said.

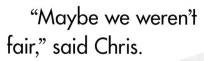

"Maybe we weren't
fair," said Chris.

"Jude doesn't play fair," said Diego. "He always fouls."

"Maybe he doesn't know how to play," said Chris. "Maybe he doesn't know the rules. Let's show him."

The next day, Jude came to the gym. The other three boys asked him to play.

"I thought you didn't want to play with me anymore," Jude said.

"We do," said Chris, "but only if you can play fair. We thought we would teach you. Playing defense means squatting down and shuffling when I'm dribbling."

"If you want to steal the ball, you reach in," said Ty. "But you can touch only the ball."

Diego got ready to shoot. "If you want to stop my shot," he said, "reach your arms straight to the sky. When I let go of the ball, then you can try to stop it."

"I get it," said Jude. "Thanks for showing me how to play. I haven't played basketball much. I still have a lot to learn."

The boys had fun playing basketball together. By the end of the day, Jude had his own nickname, too. From that day on, "Fair Game" played fair!

# FAIR SQUARES ACTIVITY

Sometimes people act unfairly because they're mean. But most of the time they act unfairly because they don't know how to be fair. You can help teach others the rules of being fair by making these Fair Squares.

**What You Need:**
a piece of paper
a pen

| classroom | recess |
|-----------|--------|
| lunchroom | home   |

**What You Do:**
1. Divide the piece of paper into four squares by folding it down the center horizontally and vertically. Trace the folds with the pen.
2. Label each square with one of these words: classroom, recess, lunchroom, home.
3. Under each word, make a list of four rules for being fair. For example, at recess, if someone is on the swing, and you want a turn, ask nicely.
4. Share the paper with your friends and classmates and be a Fair Square leader!

## GLOSSARY
**fair**—sticking to the rules, or not favoring one thing over another
**foul**—to break a rule in a sport

## To Learn More

### More Books to Read

Bender, Marie. *Fairness Counts*. Minneapolis: Abdo Pub., 2003.
Kyle, Kathryn. *Fairness*. Chanhassen, Minn.: Child's World, 2003.
Loewen, Nancy. *No Fair! Kids Talk About Fairness*. Minneapolis: Picture Window Books, 2003.
Small, Mary. *Being Fair*. Minneapolis: Picture Window Books, 2006.

### On the Web

FactHound offers a safe, fun way to find Web sites related to topics in this book. All of the sites on FactHound have been researched by our staff.

1. Visit www.facthound.com
2. Type in this special code: 1404842330
3. Click on the FETCH IT button.

Your trusty FactHound will fetch the best sites for you!

Look for books in the *Read-it!* Readers: Character Education series:

Fair Game (character education: fairness)
Green Park (character education: citizenship)

32